This book
belongs to:

_____

Snow White

The Prince

STARRING

The Queen

The Seven Dwarfs

This edition published by Parragon in 2007

Parragon
Queen Street House
4 Queen Street
Bath, BA1 1HE, UK

ISBN 978-1-4054-6295-2
Printed in China

Walt Disney's

Snow White

and the Seven Dwarfs

p

Once upon a time, there lived a princess called Snow White.
Snow White's father was dead, so she lived with her wicked
stepmother, the Queen.

Snow White was very beautiful. Her skin was as
white as snow, her hair as black as ebony wood,
and her lips were as red as a red, red rose.

The Queen was also very beautiful but very vain. She had a magic mirror and every day she would look into it and say:

"Magic mirror on the wall,
Who is the fairest one of all?"

The mirror would always reply:

"You, O Queen, are the
fairest of them all."

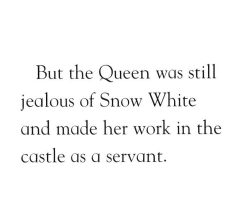

But the Queen was still jealous of Snow White and made her work in the castle as a servant.

One day, after the Queen had spoken to her magic mirror, the mirror replied:

> *"Famed is thy beauty, Majesty,*
> *But behold, a lovely maid I see.*
> *Alas, she is more fair than thee,*
> *Lips as red as a rose,*
> *Hair as black as ebony,*
> *Skin as white as snow."*

The Queen was furious. "Snow White!" she hissed. "It cannot be!"

At that very moment, Snow White was singing beside the castle well.

A handsome prince, who was passing by, stopped to listen. As soon as the Prince and Snow White saw each other, they fell in love.

When the Queen saw Snow White with the Prince, she was furious and decided to get rid of her stepdaughter.

The next morning, the Queen told her huntsman to take Snow White into the forest and kill her. "Bring back her heart to prove she is dead," she ordered.

The huntsman led the Princess into the forest but he could not kill her. He told Snow White to hide in the forest. Then he took an animal's heart to show the Queen that the Princess was dead.

Snow White wandered deep into the forest. She was
very scared but the animals led her to a little cottage. Snow
White knocked on the door and went inside. She wondered
who could live in such a tiny house.

There were seven dusty little chairs at the table. In the sink there were seven dirty spoons and bowls. And in the bedroom there were seven unmade tiny beds.

"Perhaps untidy children live here," Snow White said.

So, with the help of her forest friends, Snow White dusted and cleaned the little cottage. Then she lay across three of the tiny beds and fell asleep.

Evening came and the owners of the cottage returned. They were seven dwarfs, who worked in diamond mines, deep in the heart of the mountain. The dwarfs marched along singing:

*"Heigh-ho, heigh-ho,
It's home from work we go!"*

As soon as they entered the cottage, they knew something was wrong – it was clean! The floor had been swept and there was a delicious smell coming from a pot on the fire.

"What's happened?" they asked each other in amazement.

They searched the cottage for an intruder. They reached the bedroom just as Snow White was waking up.

"Who are you?" they asked.

"My name is Snow White," said Snow White. She explained what she was doing there. Then she asked the little men who they were.

One by one, the dwarfs introduced themselves.

"I'm Doc."
"I'm Grumpy."
"I'm Bashful."
"I'm Sleepy."
"I'm Sneezy."
"I'm Happy."
"And he's Dopey," they all shouted together.

"I'm very pleased to meet you all,"
said Snow White. "If you let me stay
here, I promise I'll look after the house
for you. I'll wash and sew and cook."
The dwarfs quickly agreed!

That evening, the cottage was filled with music and laughter.
The dwarfs sang and danced to welcome the Princess to their
home. Snow White was so happy that she soon forgot all about
her wicked stepmother.

Meanwhile, back in the castle, the wicked stepmother said the special words to the magic mirror, and the mirror replied:

"Snow White, who dwells with the seven dwarfs,
Is as fair as you and as fair again."

The Queen was furious. "Snow White must still be alive!" she screamed. She vowed to get rid of Snow White once and for all.

Down in the dungeon, the Queen cast a magic spell to disguise herself as an old pedlar woman. Then, chanting a magic spell, she dipped a bright red apple into a pot of bubbling poison.

"One bite of this and Snow White will fall into a sleep as if dead," she cackled. "Only a kiss from her true love will wake her!"

The very next day, after the dwarfs had left for work, the old pedlar woman called on Snow White selling apples.

"Try one, pretty maid," said the pedlar, handing Snow White an apple. "One bite and all your dreams will come true."

Snow White took one bite and fell to the floor as if dead.

"Now I'm the fairest in the land!" cried the wicked Queen, before fleeing.

Luckily, Snow White's forest friends had seen what had happened and went to fetch the seven dwarfs.

As the dwarfs rushed towards the cottage,
they spotted the Queen running away.
They chased her through the
forest and up the mountain.

The wicked Queen tried
to roll a huge boulder on
the dwarfs. But it rolled
back and pushed her over
the side of the mountain –
never to be seen again.

When the dwarfs returned to the cottage, they found Snow White lying on the floor as if she were dead. They could not wake her, so they took her into the forest. They placed her on a special bed and kept watch over her every day.

The months slowly passed. Snow White's bed was covered with leaves, then snow, and then the blossoms of spring. She still did not wake up.

One day, a handsome young man came riding through the forest. He was the Prince who had fallen in love with Snow White by the castle well. When he saw the Princess, he got down from his horse, leant over her and kissed her.

All at once, Snow White's eyes fluttered open.

"She's awake!" the dwarfs cried, excitedly. The wicked
Queen's spell was broken.

Before Snow White left to begin her new life with the
Prince, she kissed each of the dwarfs. "I'll come and see you
very soon," she promised them.

The dwarfs watched the Prince lead Snow White away to her new life. They knew they would miss her but they also knew that she and the Prince would live happily ever after.